W9-BAX-686

GRAPHIC WARFARE

FALLUJAH

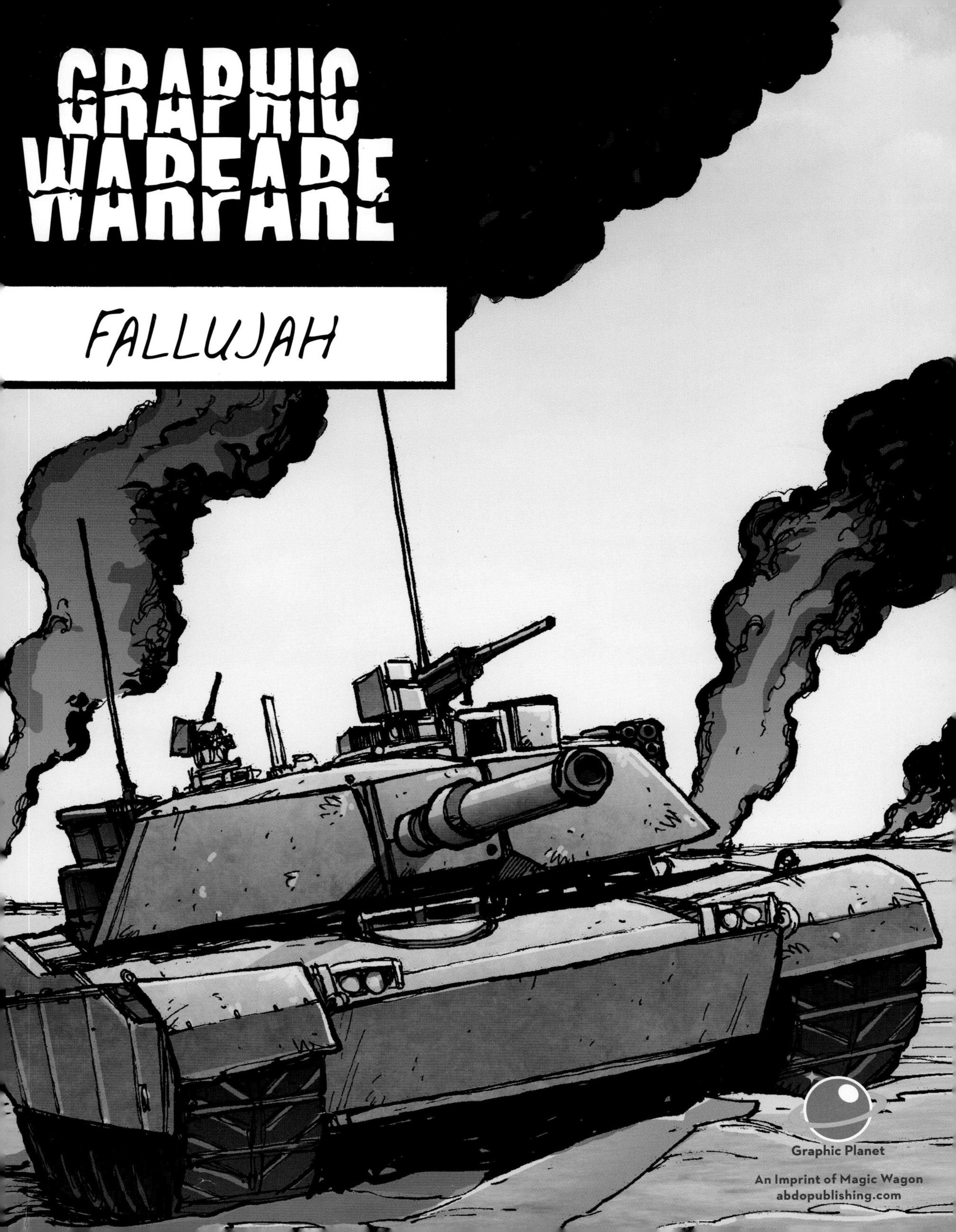

Graphic Planet

An Imprint of Magic Wagon
abdopublishing.com

Published by Magic Wagon, a division of ABDO, PO Box 398166, Minneapolis, Minnesota 55439. Copyright © 2016 by Abdo Consulting Group, Inc. International copyrights reserved in all countries. No part of this book may be reproduced in any form without written permission from the publisher. Graphic Planet™ is a trademark and logo of Magic Wagon.

Printed in the United States of America, North Mankato, Minnesota.
102015
012016

THIS BOOK CONTAINS
RECYCLED MATERIALS

Written by Joeming Dunn
Illustrated by Ben Dunn
Coloring and retouching by Robby Bevard
Lettered by Doug Dlin
Cover art by Ben Dunn
Interior layout and design by Antarctic Press
Cover design by Candice Keimig

Library of Congress Cataloging-in-Publication Data

Dunn, Joeming W.
  Fallujah / by Joeming Dunn ; illustrated by Ben Dunn.
     pages cm. -- (Graphic warfare)
  ISBN 978-1-61641-980-6
  1. Fallujah, Battle of, Fallujah, Iraq, 2004--Juvenile literature. 2. Graphic novels.
I. Dunn, Ben, illustrator. II. Title.
  DS79.764.F35D86 2016
  956.7044'342--dc23
                    2015023950

TABLE OF CONTENTS

FOREWORD

The battles of Fallujah took place in Iraq in recent times. But they are connected to hundreds of years of Middle Eastern history.

On April 25, 1920, Britain gained administration over Palestine when the League of Nations issued the British Mandate for Palestine. As Jewish people from all over the world began immigrating to the area, Palestinians were pushed from their homeland. With World War II on the horizon, Jewish immigration increased. Conflicts over land and discontent between Jews and Palestinian Arabs caused many deaths.

On May 14, 1948, the nation of Israel was established. Israel's Arab neighbors invaded. But the Arabs were unable to defeat Israel and lost more land. In addition, more Palestinians were displaced.

Arabs were committed to returning the land to the Palestinians. In the face of this threat, Israel obtained military and economic support from the United States. The United States also built military bases throughout the region to protect the oil reserves. This created a permanent American presence in the Middle East, which some Arabs resented. One of the main goals of the terrorist group Al-Qaeda is eliminating foreign presence in Muslim lands.

In addition, Islam's two branches, Sunni and Shiite, have been in conflict with each other since Muhammad's death on June 8, 632. This conflict figured in to the eight-year war between Iraq (Sunni) and Iran (Shiite), which brought great debt to Iraq.

So though they were part of the Iraq War, the battles of Fallujah were rooted in the history of the Middle East . . .

FRANCE
ROMANIA
SERBIA
BULGARIA
North Sea
GEORGIA
SPAIN
GREECE
ITALY
TURKEY
AZERBAIJAN
Caspian Sea
KAZAKHSTAN
UZBEKISTAN
KYRGYZSTAN
TURKMENISTAN
TAJIKISTAN
SYRIA
LEBANON
Mediterranean Sea
ISRAEL
JORDAN
IRAQ
IRAN
AFGHANISTAN
PAKISTAN
NEPAL
ALGERIA
LIBYA
EGYPT
SAUDI ARABIA
Persian Gulf
INDIA
MALI
NIGER
CHAD
SUDAN
Red Sea
ERITREA
OMAN
YEMEN
Arabian Sea
BURKINA FASO
NIGERIA
DJIBOUTI
Gulf of Aden
BENIN
ETHIOPIA
SOMALIA
SRI LANKA

THE MIDDLE EAST IS A REGION OF THE WORLD THAT INCLUDES WESTERN ASIA AND PART OF AFRICA.

THE HISTORY OF THE MIDDLE EAST GOES BACK TO ANCIENT TIMES. IT HAS OFTEN BEEN THE CENTER OF WORLD AFFAIRS.

IT IS ALSO KNOWN AS THE RELIGIOUS BIRTHPLACE OF JUDAISM, CHRISTIANITY, AND ISLAM.

DUE TO ITS STRATEGIC LOCATION AND ITS DIVERSE RELIGIOUS AND POLITICAL GROUPS, IT HAS ALWAYS BEEN A REGION OF CONFLICTS.

IN THE 1900S, THE MIDDLE EAST WAS DISCOVERED TO HAVE VAST RESERVES OF CRUDE OIL. THIS GAVE THE REGION A NEW ECONOMIC IMPORTANCE.

IN JULY 1979, SADDAM HUSSEIN BECAME PRESIDENT OF IRAQ.

ON SEPTEMBER 2, 1980, IRAQ INVADED IRAN. IRAQ WANTED CONTROL OF KHUZESTAN, AN OIL-RICH AREA ALONG THE BORDER. THE FIGHTING ENDED IN 1988 WITH NO CLEAR WINNER.

TURKEY

SYRIA

Tigris River

Euphrates River

IRAN

IRAQ

SAUDI ARABIA

Khuzestan

Persian Gulf

KUWAIT

AFTER THE WAR, IRAQ WAS HEAVILY IN DEBT. THEN, HUSSEIN CLAIMED THAT KUWAIT WAS ACTUALLY IRAQI TERRITORY. HE DEMANDED ITS RETURN. KUWAIT'S OIL WOULD GO A LONG WAY IN PAYING IRAQ'S WAR DEBT.

ON AUGUST 2, 1990, IRAQI FORCES INVADED KUWAIT.

THE REST OF THE WORLD CONDEMNED THE INVASION. SOON, THE UNITED NATIONS DEMANDED THAT IRAQ WITHDRAW. BUT PRESIDENT HUSSEIN IGNORED THEM.

ON JANUARY 17, 1991, OPERATION DESERT STORM, ALSO KNOWN AS THE PERSIAN GULF WAR, BEGAN. A LARGE COALITION OF MILITARY FORCES FROM MANY COUNTRIES BEGAN THEIR ATTACK ON IRAQI FORCES.

OVERWHELMED BY THE LARGE FORCE, IRAQ WAS DEFEATED WITHIN 100 HOURS OF THE GROUND ATTACK. THE CONFLICT ENDED IN FEBRUARY.

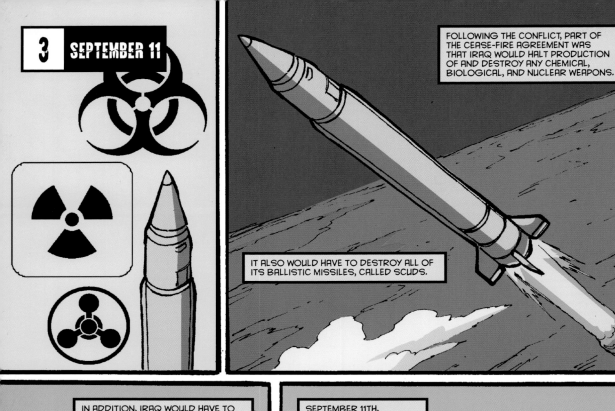

3 SEPTEMBER 11

FOLLOWING THE CONFLICT, PART OF THE CEASE-FIRE AGREEMENT WAS THAT IRAQ WOULD HALT PRODUCTION OF AND DESTROY ANY CHEMICAL, BIOLOGICAL, AND NUCLEAR WEAPONS.

IT ALSO WOULD HAVE TO DESTROY ALL OF ITS BALLISTIC MISSILES, CALLED SCUDS.

IN ADDITION, IRAQ WOULD HAVE TO ALLOW INSPECTORS TO ENSURE THE AGREEMENT WOULD BE ENFORCED. FOR THE NEXT SEVERAL YEARS, THERE WAS AN UNEASY TRUCE BETWEEN THE UNITED STATES AND IRAQ.

SEPTEMBER 11TH, 2001 . . . NEW YORK CITY, NEW YORK.

ON THAT MORNING, A SERIES OF ATTACKS LAUNCHED BY A TERRORIST ORGANIZATION CALLED AL-QAEDA HIJACKED FOUR PASSENGER PLANES. THEY USED TWO OF THEM TO DESTROY THE TWIN TOWERS OF THE WORLD TRADE CENTER.

THE TERRORISTS CRASHED A THIRD PLANE INTO THE PENTAGON IN WASHINGTON, DC. A FOURTH PLANE CRASHED IN PENNSYLVANIA AFTER ITS PASSENGERS TRIED TO RETAKE IT. THE ATTACKS RESULTED IN ALMOST 3,000 DEATHS.

AL-QAEDA WAS LED BY A SAUDI ARABIAN NAMED OSAMA BIN LADEN.

THE GROUP CARRIED OUT ITS OPERATIONS FROM THE MOUNTAINS ALONG THE AFGHANISTAN-PAKISTAN BORDER.

FOLLOWING THE ATTACKS, PRESIDENT GEORGE W. BUSH PLEDGED TO DEFEND AMERICA FROM THESE ACTS OF TERRORISM.

4 GOING TO WAR

ON OCTOBER 7, 2001, THE UNITED STATES AND SOME ALLIES BEGAN OPERATION ENDURING FREEDOM.

IT WAS A SERIES OF ATTACKS ON AFGHANISTAN TO CAPTURE OSAMA BIN LADEN AND DESTROY THE AL-QAEDA NETWORK.

IRAQ WAS SOON DRAWN INTO THE CONFLICT.

MANY BELIEVED THAT SADDAM HUSSEIN SUPPORTED OSAMA BIN LADEN AND AL-QAEDA.

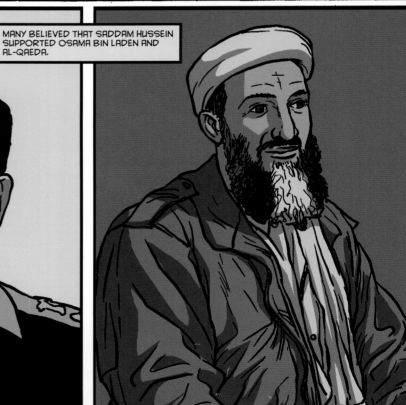

IT WAS ALSO CLAIMED THAT IRAQ POSSESSED WEAPONS OF MASS DESTRUCTION.

THIS WAS A VIOLATION OF THE UNITED NATIONS AGREEMENT FROM THE PERSIAN GULF WAR.

IN HIS 2003 STATE OF THE UNION ADDRESS, PRESIDENT BUSH OUTLINED HIS REASONS FOR INVADING IRAQ AND OUSTING SADDAM HUSSEIN.

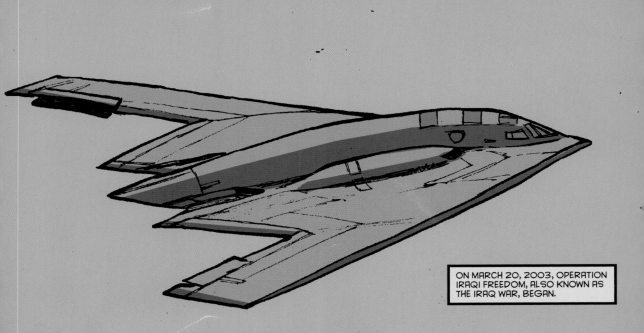

ON MARCH 20, 2003, OPERATION IRAQI FREEDOM, ALSO KNOWN AS THE IRAQ WAR, BEGAN.

THE OBJECTIVES OF THE INVASION WERE QUICKLY MET, AS THE US AND ITS ALLIES OVERWHELMED IRAQI FORCES.

BY APRIL 9, 2003, IRAQ'S CAPITAL, BAGHDAD, HAD FALLEN AND SADDAM HUSSEIN'S RULE WAS ENDED.

MISSION ACCOMPL

ON MAY 1, 2003, ON THE USS *ABRAHAM LINCOLN*, PRESIDENT BUSH DECLARED THE END OF MAJOR COMBAT OPERATIONS IN IRAQ, DECLARING "MISSION ACCOMPLISHED."

OPERATIONS AGAINST THE IRAQI MILITARY HAD OFFICIALLY ENDED. BUT THERE WERE STILL SIGNIFICANT POCKETS OF RESISTANCE FROM REBELS, ALSO CALLED INSURGENTS.

THE INSURGENTS USED GUERRILLA WARFARE, IN WHICH COMBATANTS OPERATED IN SMALL GROUPS BY USING HIT-AND-RUN TACTICS.

THEIR WEAPONS OF CHOICE INCLUDED MORTARS, CAR BOMBS, AND IMPROVISED EXPLOSIVE DEVICES (IEDS).

FALLUJAH IS A CITY IN THE IRAQI PROVINCE OF AL ANBAR. IT IS ABOUT 40 MILES (64 KM) WEST OF BAGHDAD.

DURING THE IRAQI INVASION, FALLUJAH WAS MOSTLY SPARED FROM ATTACK.

AFTER THE FALL OF THE IRAQI GOVERNMENT, THE LOCAL GOVERNMENT OF FALLUJAH WAS CONSIDERED TO BE MOSTLY SUPPORTIVE OF THE AMERICAN MILITARY.

THIS SUPPORT WAS SHORT-LIVED. ON APRIL 28, 2003, US TROOPS CONFRONTED IRAQI PROTESTORS WHO WERE DEMANDING THE REOPENING OF A SCHOOL.

WHILE THEY TRIED TO DISPERSE THE CROWD, SHOTS WERE REPORTEDLY FIRED, AND IN THE RESULTING CHAOS, 17 CIVILIANS WERE KILLED.

THE VIOLENCE CONTINUED, MOSTLY AIMED AT THE IRAQI POLICE FORCE.

AS THE ATTACKS BECAME MORE FREQUENT, ONE PARTICULAR STRIKE OCCURRED ON MARCH 31, 2004.

IN THE ATTACK, FOUR AMERICANS WHO WORKED FOR A PRIVATE MILITARY CONTRACTOR IN IRAQ WERE KILLED. THEIR BODIES WERE DRAGGED FROM THEIR VEHICLE AND MISTREATED.

IN RESPONSE TO THE KILLING, INVASION FORCES FELT THEY SHOULD TRY TO GET COMPLETE CONTROL OF FALLUJAH. TO CAPTURE THE CITY, OPERATION VIGILANT RESOLVE BEGAN ON APRIL 4, 2004.

THEIR FIRST ACTION WAS TO SURROUND AND BLOCKADE THE CITY.

THIS RESTRICTED TRAVEL TO AND FROM THE AREA.

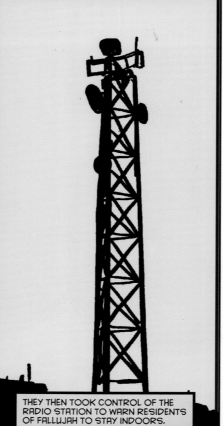

THEY THEN TOOK CONTROL OF THE RADIO STATION TO WARN RESIDENTS OF FALLUJAH TO STAY INDOORS.

MANY DECIDED TO FLEE THE CITY INSTEAD OF TAKING THE RISK OF STAYING.

THIS TACTIC ALLOWED MANY OF THE INSURGENTS IN THE CITY TO FORTIFY THEIR POSITIONS AND STOCKPILE WEAPONS.

ALLIED AIR GUNSHIPS BOMBARDED POSITIONS HELD BY THE INSURGENTS.

THE FIGHTING THEN WENT FROM DOOR TO DOOR.

SNIPERS WERE ALSO POSITIONED THROUGHOUT THE CITY TO ATTACK POCKETS OF RESISTANCE.

DURING THE EARLY STAGES OF THE OPERATION, TROOPS SUCCEEDED IN TAKING CONTROL OF KEY PARTS OF THE CITY.

HOWEVER, INSURGENT STRONGHOLDS REMAINED.

THERE WAS ALSO A CIVILIAN TOLL. MANY INNOCENTS WERE CAUGHT IN THE CROSSFIRE.

SOME PEOPLE IN THE UNITED STATES STARTED TO CHANGE THEIR MINDS ABOUT THE WAR. THIS BATTLE WAS THE FIRST ONE AGAINST INSURGENTS, RATHER THAN AGAINST THE IRAQI MILITARY, WHO WERE LOYAL TO SADDAM HUSSEIN.

ON APRIL 9, 2004, A CEASE-FIRE WAS ORDERED IN THE HOPES OF MAKING IT EASIER TO HOLD NEGOTIATIONS BETWEEN ALL THE PARTIES.

THE CEASE-FIRE ALLOWED SUPPLIES AND HUMANITARIAN AID TO ENTER THE CITY.

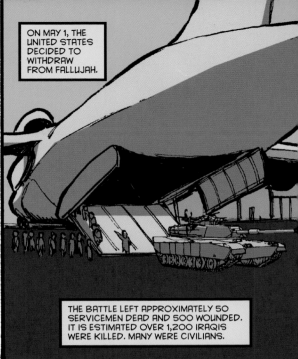

ON MAY 1, THE UNITED STATES DECIDED TO WITHDRAW FROM FALLUJAH.

THE BATTLE LEFT APPROXIMATELY 50 SERVICEMEN DEAD AND 500 WOUNDED. IT IS ESTIMATED OVER 1,200 IRAQIS WERE KILLED. MANY WERE CIVILIANS.

THE SECURITY OF THE REGION WAS TURNED OVER TO MUHAMMED LATIF. HE WOULD BE IN CHARGE OF A BRIGADE MADE OF IRAQIS. IT WAS BELIEVED THEY COULD STOP THE RISE OF THE INSURGENCY.

THE BRIGADE UNIT ULTIMATELY FAILED AND COLLAPSED. AND, INSURGENTS OBTAINED AMERICAN WEAPONS THAT HAD BEEN LEFT TO THE BRIGADE.

6 SECOND BATTLE

THE INSURGENT LEADER WAS BELIEVED TO BE ABU MUSAB AL-ZARQAWI. THE INSURGENCY HAD GROWN TO INCLUDE 4,000 TO 5,000 MEMBERS. MOST OF THEM WERE NON-IRAQIS.

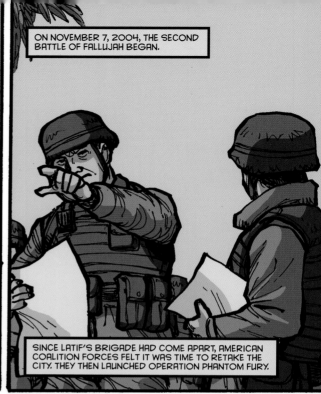

ON NOVEMBER 7, 2004, THE SECOND BATTLE OF FALLUJAH BEGAN.

SINCE LATIF'S BRIGADE HAD COME APART, AMERICAN COALITION FORCES FELT IT WAS TIME TO RETAKE THE CITY. THEY THEN LAUNCHED OPERATION PHANTOM FURY.

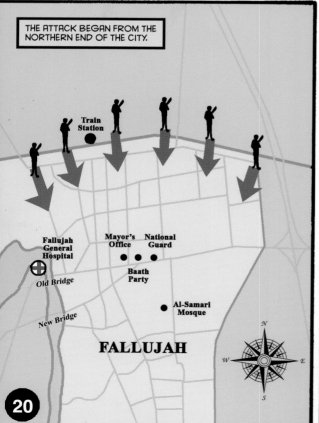

THE ATTACK BEGAN FROM THE NORTHERN END OF THE CITY.

Train Station

Fallujah General Hospital

Mayor's Office National Guard

Baath Party

Old Bridge

Al-Samari Mosque

New Bridge

FALLUJAH

THE FIRST PHASE WAS TO SECURE THE BRIDGES AND ROADS TO PREVENT ANY INSURGENT ESCAPES.

US FORCES TOOK CONTROL OF THE CITY'S POWER GRID.

BETWEEN THE FIRST AND SECOND BATTLES, THE INSURGENTS HAD PREPARED FOR THE ATTACK AND STRENGTHENED THEIR DEFENSES BY BUILDING TUNNELS.

THEY ALSO CONSTRUCTED AND USED A VARIETY OF IEDS.

BUILT WITH SIMPLE ITEMS SUCH AS PROPANE TANKS, OIL BARRELS, OR EVEN SODA BOTTLES, THESE WERE PLACED IN BUILDINGS AND TRIGGERED REMOTELY WHEN TROOPS ENTERED.

THE FIGHTING WAS FIERCE, ESPECIALLY IN THIS URBAN SETTING, WHERE ATTACKS SOMETIMES OCCURRED HOUSE TO HOUSE.

TO AVOID TRAPS SET UP BY THE INSURGENTS, TANKS RAMMED HOLES INTO SUSPECTED HOUSES.

DESPITE THE HEAVY FIGHTING, ABOUT 70 PERCENT OF THE CITY WAS UNDER COALITION CONTROL BY MID-NOVEMBER.

COALITION TROOPS SEIZED LARGE AMOUNTS OF WEAPONS AND EXPLOSIVES THROUGHOUT THE CITY.

BY THE END OF NOVEMBER, MOST OF THE CITY WAS UNDER AMERICAN COALITION CONTROL. ABU MUSAB AL-ZARQAWI ESCAPED CAPTURE.

AT THE END OF MAJOR OPERATIONS IN FALLUJAH, MORE THAN 100 COALITION FORCES HAD BEEN KILLED IN ACTION, INCLUDING OVER 50 AMERICANS. IT IS ESTIMATED THAT 1,200 TO 1,400 INSURGENTS WERE KILLED DURING THE BATTLE.

IN MID-DECEMBER, RESIDENTS WERE ALLOWED BACK INTO THE CITY. AT THIS POINT, ABOUT 25 PERCENT OF THE CITY HAD SUSTAINED EXTENSIVE DAMAGE.

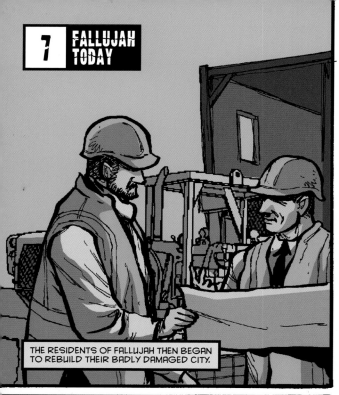

THE RESIDENTS OF FALLUJAH THEN BEGAN TO REBUILD THEIR BADLY DAMAGED CITY.

THOUGH THE CITY WAS TAKEN, MANY DID NOT CONSIDER IT A DECISIVE VICTORY.

THEY BELIEVED THAT AL-ZARQAWI AND MANY OF THE NON-IRAQI INSURGENTS LEFT BEFORE THE ASSAULT.

THE INSURGENCY STARTED TO USE DIFFERENT TACTICS. THEY AVOIDED OPEN BATTLES AND ADOPTED MORE STRATEGIC ATTACKS TO AVOID LARGE LOSSES.

EVEN THOUGH THE CITY ITSELF WAS UNDER COALITION CONTROL, THE SURROUNDING AREAS STILL HAD EXTENSIVE INSURGENT ACTIVITY.

EVENTUALLY, ALL MILITARY CONTROL WAS GIVEN TO THE PROVINCIAL GOVERNMENT OF IRAQ.

ALMOST ALL US TROOPS WERE WITHDRAWN FROM IRAQ BY THE END OF 2011.

THE IRAQ WAR HAS REMAINED A SUBJECT OF MUCH CONTROVERSY.

MANY QUESTION THE JUSTIFICATION AND THE COST OF THE WAR, SINCE WEAPONS OF MASS DESTRUCTION WERE NEVER FOUND.

DESPITE THE REMOVAL OF SADDAM HUSSEIN AS THE DICTATOR OF IRAQ, VIOLENCE BETWEEN DIFFERENT FACTIONS IN THE COUNTRY REMAINS.

THE POLITICAL SITUATION IS STILL UNSTABLE.

HOWEVER, WE WILL NOT FORGET THOSE WHO SACRIFICED THEIR LIVES IN FALLUJAH.

MAP

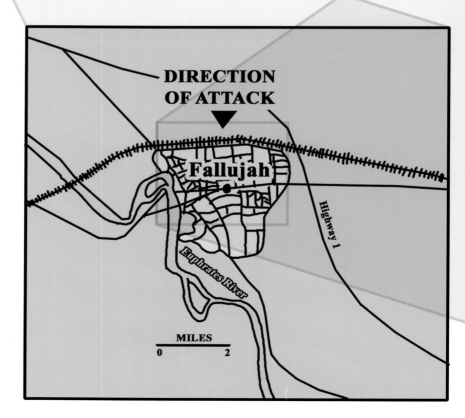

DIRECTION OF ATTACK

Fallujah

Euphrates River

Highway 1

MILES
0   2

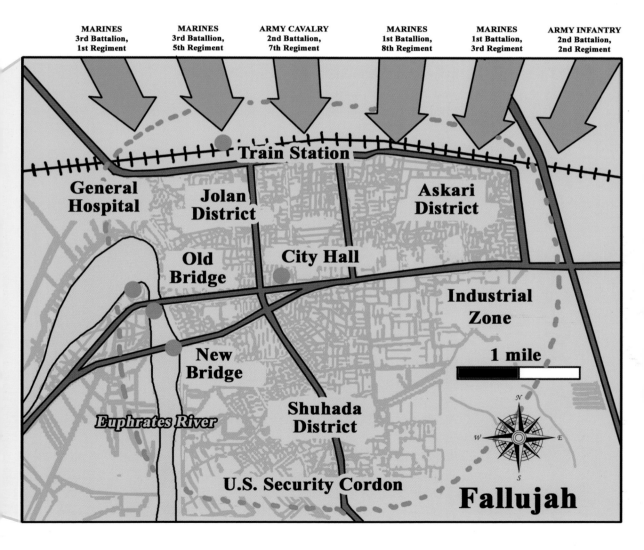

MARINES
3rd Battalion,
1st Regiment

MARINES
3rd Batallion,
5th Regiment

ARMY CAVALRY
2nd Battalion,
7th Regiment

MARINES
1st Battalion,
8th Regiment

MARINES
1st Battalion,
3rd Regiment

ARMY INFANTRY
2nd Battalion,
2nd Regiment

Train Station

General
Hospital

Jolan
District

Askari
District

Old
Bridge

City Hall

Industrial
Zone

1 mile

New
Bridge

Euphrates River

Shuhada
District

U.S. Security Cordon

Fallujah

TIMELINE

632 June 8
Muhammad died, and conflict over his successor caused Islam's split into Sunni and Shiite groups.

1900s
Middle East oil reserves were discovered.

1920 April 25
Britain gained administration over Palestine.

1948 May 14
The nation of Israel was established; Arabs vowed to take back the land for Palestine.

1979 July
Saddam Hussein became president of Iraq.

1980 September 2
The Iran-Iraq war began.

1990 August 2
Iraq invaded Kuwait.

1991 January 17
Operation Desert Storm began.

2001 September 11
Al-Qaeda terrorists attacked the United States.

2001 October 7
Operation Enduring Freedom began.

2003 March 20
Operation Iraqi Freedom began.

2003 April 28
Violence ensued during a school opening protest in Fallujah, Iraq.

2004 April 4
First Battle of Fallujah began; five days later a cease-fire was called.

2004 November 7
Second Battle of Fallujah began.

2011
US troops were withdrawn from Iraq.

GEORGE W. BUSH
(July 6, 1946–)

George W. Bush was the forty-third president of the United States. In 1968, he graduated from Yale University. In 1975, Bush earned an MBA from Harvard Business School. Beginning in 1994, Bush served two terms as Republican governor of Texas. He was elected president of the United States in 2000. On September 11, 2001, President Bush led the nation through the worst terror attack on American soil, and declared a global War on Terror. In 2003, Bush turned his attention to Iraq, where President Saddam Hussein was defying United Nations sanctions. On March 20, 2003, the Iraq War began when a coalition led by the US and Britain invaded Iraq. The November 2004 Battle of Fallujah was the bloodiest battle of the war.

SADDAM HUSSEIN
(April 28, 1937–December 30, 2006)

Saddam Hussein was president of Iraq from 1979 until 2003. In 1957, he joined the revolutionary Ba'th Party, which came to power in 1968. In 1980, President Hussein's forces attacked Iran, leading to the Iran-Iraq war, which ended in 1988. Two years later, Iraq invaded Kuwait, and the Persian Gulf War began in January 1991. One month later, United Nations forces defeated Iraq. Strict sanctions were implemented against the country, including destruction of weapons. Hussein later ended cooperation with UN weapons inspectors, leading to the March 20, 2003, invasion by a coalition led by the United States and Britain. On December 13, Hussein was captured. He was tried and convicted of several charges. Hussein was executed on December 30, 2003.

QUICK STATS

Iraq War

Dates:
March 20, 2003–
December 15, 2011

Number of Casualties:

For the Coalition:
41,606

Estimated For Iraq:
500,000

Belligerents:

Coalition Forces including United States, the United Kingdom, Australia

Iraq

Important Leaders:

For the Coalition: US president George W. Bush, British prime minister Tony Blair

For Iraq: Iraqi president Saddam Hussein, Iraqi Major General Muhammed Latif, Insurgent leader Abu Musab al-Zarqawi

GLOSSARY

allies
people, groups, or nations united for some special purpose.

blockade
the cutting off of an area by soldiers or ships. A blockade prevents supplies and people from going into or out of an area.

brigade
a military group composed of a headquarters, one or more infantry or armor groups, and support groups.

cease-fire
a temporary stopping of hostile activities.

civilian
a person who is not an active member of the military.

coalition
a temporary group of different peoples or states joined for a common cause.

debt
something owed to someone, especially money.

diverse
made up of unlike pieces or qualities.

economic
relating to the production and use of goods and services.

negotiate
to work out an agreement about the terms of something.

Operation Desert Storm
the US name for the Persian Gulf War. A group of 39 countries joined to liberate Kuwait from Iraqi forces. The conflict lasted from January 16 to February 28, 1991.

province
a political division of a country.

strategic
relating to a plan that is created to achieve a goal.

truce
an agreement between opposing forces to stop fighting.

United Nations
a group of nations formed in 1945. Its goals are peace, human rights, security, and social and economic development.

urban
of or relating to a city.

violate
to do something that is not allowed.

WEBSITES

To learn more about Graphic Warfare, visit booklinks.abdopublishing.com.
These links are routinely monitored and updated to provide the most current

INDEX